A GLASS OF WATER

A Collection of Poetry and Prose

JORRY LUZ

A Glass of Water
Copyright © 2022 by Jorry Luz

Tellwell Talent
www.tellwell.ca

ISBN
978-0-2288-6416-5 (Paperback)
978-0-2288-6417-2 (eBook)

To my nanay and tatay
Thank you for believing in me

Contents

Introduction

Is the glass half full, or half empty?

This is a metaphor that has been posed as a question to divide people into two separate groups: the pessimists and optimists. This dichotomy never made much sense to me because to believe that one's experiences and perspective can somehow be encapsulated in some binary answer seemed too simple, and I don't think life is that simple. I feel like humanity deserves more credit for how complex we all are. To add more nuance to this metaphor, I've decided to remove the distinction amongst the two perspectives and created my own take on that saying.

The end of an era becomes the breeding ground for change. And it's inevitable to have to say goodbye to people and experiences, storing them away into the past. Now there exists a gap in our lives where a piece of our past once lived—a place that might feel as if it's empty, but I don't really think it is. As an engineering student, I learned early on that cold doesn't exist; it is rather the absence of heat. So, what if the same applies to life? This part isn't empty but rather an absence of the familiarity we've grown to be fond of.

I don't really see life as being half full or half empty, but instead always filled to the brim. Half filled with water, half with air. Life will always be full; whether it's full of joy, full of pain, full of love, or full of crap, it will always be full. People meet their demise thinking they never lived a full life because they filled it with things that didn't feel worthwhile, but the thing is, life was always full to begin with.

I first wrote this concept a little after I said farewell to the bittersweet prologue of life that we call high school. I've reread what I wrote multiple times to remind myself of an innocent type of wisdom, one that was rooted in perspective but not experience. A lesson my younger self understood more than I do now. This book is a mixed drink, and instead of using the Optimist and the Pessimist as my ingredients, I've instead made it with equal parts Realist and Dreamer—the two different people I had personified over the years. Using these perspectives, you'll see how the ideas of love, heartbreak, beauty, life, death, and humanity intermingle with each other in this glass in unexpected ways.

I hope this collection can show you that a Realist isn't just a pessimist, and a Dreamer isn't just an optimist. That we as humans carry so much depth in the small parts that make us whole and, in the end, maybe I'll convince you of the fullness that life has to offer. Many of these poems carry ideas and lessons that meant something to me once upon a time, so I hope they might find a way to mean something to you.

I know sometimes it gets hard to breathe
What I like to do when that happens
Is to slow down
And grab
A Glass of Water.

An Opening Breath

A Glass of Water

I hope this meets you well
like a cold breeze in the summer
like a deep breath when you're lost
like a glass of water
when you're empty

Oh, What a Jungle

Come with me so that we may venture
and humour me for a moment.
Imagine a world in which we
fed our souls with poetry

And gave way for words
to pry open the ambivalence of life within us
to unwrap the mysteries hidden behind the breath of the living.

As we hunt for the meaning enclosed in these words
I hope that at the end of this excursion we might look backwards
to the safe passage we've created for ourselves
when we wandered into this jungle of poetry.

The Breadcrumbs I Followed

I remember seeing you across the gymnasium.
You and your ocean-like dress and wave-like hair
I found you very beautiful
but that wasn't the reason I was looking.

It was because you looked back at me
with something hidden behind your eyes.
It seemed you had an answer to a question
I hadn't thought to ask yet.

I didn't quite know what I didn't know
until I shook your hand and you spoke of your love for poetry
and the abundance of journals
that gave refuge to your thoughts.

You were a stranger that lent me the key to finding breadcrumbs
of myself
scattered along this stretch of time and I followed it here.
It's funny to think that you were just someone passing through
and what came of it was this book.

THE REALIST

hello

hello time,
why do you run so quickly?
do you ever get tired?
some days I wish you walked through the good parts,
and ran through the bad ones.
I'm told you heal—
if so, why do you carry me to death
so unapologetically?

hello space,
does it ever get tiring being the *where*
but never the *why*?
that you serve purpose without reason?
that people need you but never notice you?
nevertheless,
thank you for giving me a place to live.

hello love,
why do you feel like an echo
that has lost its strength?
a runaway with so much baggage
a half-remembered dream
and yet be the best thing that has ever happened to me.
I wonder if I'll ever see you again—
maybe you never left?

hello death,
I wonder if you're a lonely soul.
people say your voice never goes beyond a whisper,
so timid in your existence yet bold in your actions.
I've also heard that you don't mean to hurt or harm,
you are just the bridge between then and now, now and later.
I'm not afraid of you, nor am I looking forward to our
introduction.
I hope that when we finally meet,
life introduces us with care and grace.

Tied

I'm told that I was born with a tongue two sizes too small—
but in reality, it's no smaller than yours,
the only difference is the extra piece of skin
that ties my tongue to the bottom of my mouth.

A destiny of silence lodged in my head
as I was set on mute from the beginning.

Luckily by the age of two I said my first words
by the age of three I was able to string together
the dots of voices in my head and teach them to yearn for air
and by the age of four you couldn't stop me.

My mouth was a waterfall of surprising sounds
overflowing with the longing to be heard.

But…

We grow up to tie our voices to the backs of our mouths
brimming with the ability to
manifest conversations with brick walls.

We train the words that run marathons in our minds
to maintain a world afraid
of change, the strange, the ugly.

Leading us to tame the lionesses of thoughts we bear
with two ounces of half-grown courage
as if courage can be found at the bottom of a shot glass.

I look at the irony that I am where I first started—
someone with voices imitating the way I sound.
How did I get back here?

How in the world did I unlearn to speak my truth?
Once more that little boy with a big voice
who wasn't supposed to have a voice at all.

Speak Slowly

Speak slowly,
your thoughts may move faster than your tongue
they argue with the tempo
of the words you let out.

Speak slowly,
with intention
because no one will listen
if your words are born from unfinished thoughts.

Speak slowly,
so that the momentum of your words
can be stopped at a moment's notice
when the world is urging you

to listen.

read this with a whisper

i am all the things you have trouble admitting to yourself
i am all the awkward mistakes and interactions that feel like
nails on a chalkboard
i am all your "i love yous" too important to be told to anyone
but one
i am a whisper

i carry words your mouth is too shy to share
i let you believe that the world is deaf to your voice
i am a deterrent and skill
i am an enemy but friend
i am a whisper

Read This Out Loud

I am everything you aren't afraid to be
I am the speeches and advice you claim as yours
I am nothing but strong and vibrant
But I make mistakes
I think a little less
I'm too ambitious for my own good

I am you
Living out loud

I am you
Searching for a way
To survive a world
Full of noise

Fever

I have a fever
with no cure to settle me
but a mother's love

Maraming Salamat Po

I wonder if my parents would love me more if I spoke their
native tongue
because sometimes I feel like a stranger in my own house
pretending to ignore the dinner table conversations.

> They call on me, "Jorry, are you listening?"
> I look up, a burdened smile following me as I say,
> "Sorry, I wasn't—"

But I was—head down, ears astute, mending fragments of stories
in hopes that this thread might lead me to a better understanding.
I recite to myself one phrase, "maraming salamat po,"
meaning "thank you very much,"

because I need them to know in their language
how thankful I am to have been brought to this country.
The echo repeats in my head, "maraming salamat po."

Hoping that when my voice deems it worthy
to be said out loud, I will not be swept away
with their laughter like a child would be.

A reminder that I don't belong in the skin I was born with:
the life between belonging here and not.
I want to know how it feels to know who you are—

to know your roots without any memories, a history before
your birth,
to know your place on a tree when your leaf doesn't match.

The last time we visited the Philippines
I saw how my dad spoke to the kids there;
they understood each other.

There was a harmony in the conversations
my father had with these strangers;
and that's why I stopped making fun of my dad's accent at the
dinner table—

I never want him to carry misplaced shame
for a language and a culture I so desperately want to be part of.

Embrace

I miss embraces

that became competitions

for who could squeeze the tightest—

who could hug the hurt away

Can I Tell You a Funny Story?

Before I was born
my parents believed I was a girl
because a certain male defining attribute
was *way* too small in the ultrasound.
Unfortunately, I came out a boy...

There it is.
Exactly what I was looking for.
The faint smile that lifts the
heavy edges of your mouth with ease
that pushes this defensive facade away.

You've slowly forgotten how to smile by instinct
and instead you do so by choice;
but you haven't had the opportunity to do so lately.

That smile, it floated to the top of your tough exterior—
I saw it drowning
        in your doubts
        in your worries
        in your insecurities.

The unsuppressed delight
dancing through the crinkles by your eyes
running through your cheeks as they bloom
and arriving at that breathtaking smile.

Thank you for letting me see it.

Shadow

I don't think it's uncommon to be afraid of your own shadow
the twilight projecting a flawed mirror image

But
when darkness falls onto my life
and I see a light ahead of me
as I walk toward it
I want to convince my shadow
that I'm worth following

Revered

It's difficult to imagine
that those I revere
were once fearful little children
as I am today

To the Woman Who Taught Me Gratitude

You would start every class with an oath

> "Today I will learn something new—"
> a phrase not easily forgotten
> and I can say for certain
> people still remember

and end every day with a conversation.

> "Sit down everyone, let's talk about the meaning of life—"
> an invitation to conversations
> in which you shared your observations
> of what mattered most in the world.

I would give anything to remember verbatim
the wisdom you spoke into existence
the kindness you carried in your heart
the wit that made everyone smile.

* * *

Ms. Falsetto was a curly-haired Italian woman who never
seemed to age.
She had a smile that could pierce through early morning classes
and jokes that would give birth
to a murmur of awkward laughter.

The kinds of jokes that were better with age—
the ones best heard in a memory
bringing you delayed laughter
as you remember just how awfully great they were.

She was a woman whose personality
and vibrance shook a room.
Her skin was fair and young
her eyes easy to trust
her voice elegant but firm—
there was so much to appreciate
you barely would have noticed
that she used a walker every day.

Although her hands firmly gripped the plastic handlebars that
let her stand—
a slight tremor with every step she took—
there was nothing about her that said she felt sorry for herself.
She had the kind of dedication of putting one foot forward
in every sense of the phrase, footsteps I'd been honoured to follow.

She didn't walk that fast
and it took her longer than most to traverse the school;
but my goodness she had a way with words.
She filled the time she walked with conversations and stories
that she told to students who were near enough to hear them.

Her lectures were composed of fireworks
that bore sparks to ignite the most
uninterested of students with the passion to learn.
And on top of it all she had a gaze—
not a stare not a scowl nor glare.

She had a gaze that spoke volumes to staff and student alike.
It meant "I believe you can do this."
She could somehow tear down the adversity
that lived in most people
with only one look.

I wish I wrote notes
on the lectures she gave to us after hours.
The lectures that made us
think about the kind of people we were meant to be—
simultaneously gifting us direction and autonomy.

I once had a conversation with her about
what made life seem unfair.
In what seemed to feel like only a few words
she taught me about gratitude.

She explained to me the intricacies
of being grateful for the little things in life
and that the delay of gratitude
only bears better fruits to harvest
only ensures better aged wine
only carries better stories to be told.

When I left her class for the last time
she gifted me a book and a lovely goodbye letter.
To this day I haven't finished this book.
Not for lack of trying, but because
I'm afraid once I reach the last word on that last page—
the best teacher I've ever had—
the woman who taught me gratitude
will have nothing more to teach me.

I hope one day
I'll have the courage
to finish this book
but for now
I think I'll remain as her student—
because every day I promise to learn something new
and I hope at the end
I'd find the meaning of life
that she spoke so fondly of.

Upside Down

When I was in kindergarten
during silent reading I sat next to the smartest kid in class
I couldn't read yet so I opened my book upside down—
imitating the slight head turn of my colleague that could read

from then on, I always believed that I'd follow in the footsteps
of others
that all I'd ever be was secondary
all I'd ever do was typical
anything but original

Realize

Just because you have a passion for something
doesn't mean you can make it a career

Just because you work hard
doesn't mean you'll succeed

Just because you fall in love with someone
doesn't mean you'll end up together

Reality is just a tyrant
winding up his swing to show you just how heavy his hand can be

That Moment in the Morning

I am at my happiest when I wake up
because for just a brief moment I forget
that you're no longer in my life

Then like a heavy wave
reality crashes in
looking for revenge

Too Much

First you say
I love you too much

And then you say
"I love you" too much

End

Four times already
I have allowed myself
to remain helpless in the face of love
and I just do not know
if my heart can stretch any further.

I used to think
when you fell in love
you took a knife to the heart
and cut a patch as an offering
in hopes that someone would watch over it.

Instead of this
I now believe
that when you fall in love
you give them just the end of a thread.
I think we do this so that when we're lost
we can always find our way back
to the person we love.

I've watched my heart unravel to the ends of the earth
in four different directions.
Nowadays when I'm lost
I check if my heart is still there—
if there is any more string left to give
and if there is any more string left to follow.

Knot

There is a knot around your heart
take a moment and try to find it

The rope curving over and under
and with every word *that* person says they pull it tighter

But you're not fully convinced
of its purpose

Is this knot holding your heart in place
keeping it from falling apart?

Or preventing it from beating
stopping it from loving?

A Poisoned Idea

I was once left in the dark
as you pronounced your thoughts.
A time when all I could do was wait
and trust that you'd come back to me.

I look back on those moments now,
and little did I know, in what felt like an instant
we were both poisoned with an idea—
two sides of a coin that would never be able to see face to face.

An idea: the most destructive thing ever known
        able to crumble governments and countries
        to corrupt man in the wake of inspiration
        and poison passion

You had convinced yourself you should come back.
I had convinced myself I should leave.

Torture

Today I walked by all the places there used to be an us
and I followed the fading footsteps of these two past lovers.
I watched them as the memories we left
in the wake of our declining love pierced my eyes.

I see what you see—
I see the torture I've put you through
and I'm sorry.

Apologies

I apologize to the man after me
I too remember how the scent of her past lover lingered faintly.
I could still see the impression on her heart
written with his initials.

I apologize that you next
will have to bear the reminder of our shortcomings as men
and be invited to fill in the blanks, crevices, and holes I left in her.

Love Song

You never wrote me a love song
you only ever wrote of the ways I didn't love you enough

Music with a playful melody to distract
from my mistakes
and the blemishes that ruin
the illusion of perfect love

But although you never wrote me a love song
I know you still tried your best
to write us the perfect love story

Cries in the Wind

I cry to you at night
but it'll never reach
your ears.

My voice will dampen
in the wind and soften
from my fears.

I hope the echo of
my life reverberates
your sea.

But never disturbs
the water's surface—
so as still, she still can be.

Only at the End

During the day, we forget to thank our lungs for working so hard to keep us breathing.
During the day, we don't let our eyes appreciate what they see.
During the day, we treat the sound that flows in our ears as sewage and not a bountiful river.

At the end of the day when the sun packs it in
and the moon fills the sky like an old friend—
only then do we understand what it feels like
to not have something we had before.

Only at the end do we realize
that one's absence is felt more strongly
than their presence ever will.

After You

There was a *before you*
and now there's an *after you*
two parts of a story
I can't quite fully grasp

Broken Keyboard

Myself alone co_ldn't f_n_sh th_s poem
beca_se the letters,
" __ "
and
" __ "
no longer work.

_t's as tho_gh my comp_ter _s secretly tell_ng me
that they can't ex_st
on the same page
anymore.

That we can no longer wr_te a story
w_th
"__" and "__"

Love as a Math Equation

Let's begin

7,594,000,000

There are about 7.594 billion people around the world.
I'm not much of a traveller
so, chances are if you're like me
you're betting on meeting someone in your own city.

675,000

For simplicity's sake
let's say half were born men
the other born women
and if you play for only one side like I do,
the sample space just got smaller.

337,500

About 7.6% of those women are about my age give or take a
couple of years.

25,650

Chances are, more than half of them are already taken.

12,825

1 in 10 I'll find attractive or interesting.

1,280

Probably only 1 in 20 would even look my way

64

That's correct, 64.
Given my record I'll probably fall in love with half of them.

32

Following that trend, how many of them would fall for me?

3

Maybe?

Out of these women
what are the chances
I screw it up somehow?

Every. Single. Time.

I could spend hours reciting the complicated rules of probability
life being at the will of randomness
entropy ruling our chances.

The concept of such a random event as love
cannot be predicted
but somehow

people still fall in love

and they make it work.
They have found a way to defy all possible reason.
They are not the proof that love prevails;

rather, they are the exception to the claim that
it's impossible.

I Hope You Read This

Through the art we create
we finally get the chance
to say all the words
we're too afraid
to say

Ruins

When we go back to the ruins in hopes to rebuild something meaningful from the rubble, where do you suggest we begin? The granite and limestone foundations have been compromised, and the columns and steel beams have rusted—how can we start to start over?

Rerun

I fell in love,
she loved me, just not in *that* way
but it's okay.

I fell in love,
she loved me, just not enough
but it's okay.

I fell in love,
she loved me, from what I could see
but it's hard to conceive
the possibility from these melancholy eyes,
but it's okay.

I fell in love,
she loved me, but just a little too late.
I already learned to convince myself
that my heart is not a football I can throw when I'm afraid,
that my feelings don't have to spill through my idiosyncrasies,
that I wasn't the guy for her.

She somehow thought otherwise,
like waiting in line at the store only to realize
you're missing that one ingredient to make a good life
but you've already been waiting in line.

What do you do now?

You give in.
Lose your spot.
Try again
and hope that whatever you're looking for
is still there where you left it.

Forgotten

I don't want to be remembered
I want to be forgotten

I want to convince my cells to disappear
while I tell them stories of when they were needed

I want to grip memories so tight
that they decide not to breathe

I don't want to be remembered
I want to be forgotten

Unapologetic

I will never apologize
          for complimenting a woman
But as a male I do apologize
          for the rest of us men who
          use compliments as
          fingertips for finagling
          zippers and buttons
I apologize for men
          who use flattery as shears
          to tear pant seams
I apologize that the
          world has betrayed your trust
          by telling you that beauty is only skin deep
          leading you to believe that what
          I have to say next isn't true

I think you are beautiful
a sculpture of complexity and stunning existence
I am in awe and adoration of women like you

How in the world am I supposed to
reach my hands through this page
hold you by the face
and convince you to believe
the tapestry of beauty that you are

We Used to Be Friends

I consider you a friend
because of our history
but you haven't been there for me
anytime recently.

There was a time when
I would've taken a bullet for you.
I remember writing it in my journal
as if it were a contract to God
promising that I'd give up my life for our friendship.

Yet right now you have no knowledge
of where I've been and who I hope to become.
You'd see my skin and only recognize the surface.
You'd say hello with an inkling of goodbyes following you.
You'd tell me, "Let's hang out soon—"
a proposal as fickle as the thin ice our friendship walks upon.

Then again, I don't know who you are either.
I'm blind to the other side of yourself
that you don't share with the rest of the world.
I have no idea what you're going through;
so, I guess I wouldn't consider you a friend anymore,
I think the word that best fits is

Stranger

Frame

I went to the copy shop today. I took two buses, walked for a bit, and printed a poster. I bought a frame from the arts and crafts store only a couple of blocks down and walked up a small hill, but this time the ground beneath me decided to betray my trust and to my dismay I slipped and fell on my poster. I saw a huge crease and a little crack in the printing and as frustrated as I was, I still fought with my emotions because of how silly it was to get mad for the ruin of a twelve-dollar poster. I decided to leave it be and frame it anyways only later to realize you can't see the creases when it's framed—

People can't see how broken you are, no matter how transparent you pass yourself up to be—
People can only see what's wrong if you let them in.

Echo

I find it strange that the emptier a room is, the more it echoes.
As if the absence isn't enough of a reminder.
The echo of these lost thoughts
reverberating through the walls of my skull
reminding me that I've forgotten something
while at the same time not letting me remember.

Was it a task?
Was it a memory?
Was it a dream?
Was it the person I used to be?

It's Daunting

being unknown at every corner I turn
being a teardrop in a sea
being a stranger in the city

First Apartment

This apartment is my world. My persona spread across the floors, my purpose placed on tabletops and memories hung on the walls. I am stuck in this universe of me, and all I have left are my thoughts to keep me company. No one to knock on my door and ask if they could be part of my universe.

I No Longer Know the Rain

I can no longer hear the gentle footsteps
that the rain used to leave on my roof.
The smooth droplets of rain running down the pavement of
my arms,
only to leap at my fingertips, every droplet stealing my warmth.

Rain was the baptism that mother nature bore for me as I
entered my youth.
A lifetime ago I would walk along the highway in hopes to be
rained on.

Although the clear skies, sudden calms and lulls in the wind
give us time to breathe,
never have I felt so alive than in a rainstorm.
There's no feeling greater than having mother nature mute your
screams so your lungs can get a taste of how loud they can
roar. A rainstorm so enthralling it allows life to crash into you
without stealing your wind.

I thought that living on a mountain would mean the rain would
meet me faster than those in troughs, but the sun has taken
control of the sky and dispersed the clouds in a way where rain
has become but a fond memory.

Looking in the Wrong Places

Did you know our oceans are over eighty percent unseen?
Yet as ambitious as we are
we've already given up
on discovering our world
and decided to set sail to other ones
in search of meaning.

We've been looking in the wrong places
our entire lives and it doesn't look like we'll ever stop.

We are so dumbstruck with the idea of exploration
that we are blinded to our obligation
to the body of land and water we claim to be ours.

We search for meaning in others
yet the oceans of our bodies

are yet to be discovered
are yet to be appreciated
are yet to be seen.

I know it's tempting to
        build ships filled with artificial air
        meant to explore outwardly.

I know it's tempting to
        place all your life support on this ship to land
        on another body hoping that this would sustain you.

But you don't need another planet—
you don't need another person
to give you meaning.

Look inwardly and start exploring
the vast unknown
that is you.

A Message to the
Meaning-Making Machines

To those who dig into life
looking for some treasure chest of meaning

not every word has to be an ingredient
to some grandiose metaphor

sometimes words are just words
sometimes things just happen
and sometimes
it is what it is

Correct

Knowledge has found a way to turn itself into ammunition for the masses.
The world now wielding weapons at each other's throats.
I miss the times in my life where not knowing simply meant that—
instead of being mistaken for "not caring."

Somehow being right is now more important than being kind,
somehow, we get drunk on our truths and forget what we're fighting for,
somehow, this generation relishes in the chaos of a battleground made with ones and zeros.

We have become a song
that no one wants to sing—
the dissonance in our existence—
the lack of harmony in our lives.

I understand what it means
to be passionate about one's truth,
I just no longer understand why we must divide ourselves in pursuit of it.

Cocktail

I lived my life trying to tell myself everyone else was going through something difficult, therefore my pain in comparison didn't matter. I convinced myself to feel numb with the words I put in other people's mouths. I listened to their lips move out of sync as I misread their emotions. I thought to myself, "I'm not allowed to be in pain, I have no right. Right?", searching for permission in the fault lines hidden in the minds of my peers.

It is evening now, and all I am left with is the excuses I've manifested into existence, designed to simply simmer in my company. I sit here, bar and stool, slowly becoming this glass filled with unanswered questions. A cocktail: one part doubtful, two parts afraid and a shot of something strange steeped in the rubble of my past self.

I find that I am best served neat.

Gravitational

We invite the trouble that enters our lives because our very existence gravitates the attention that we don't desire. A person of wealth will be hunted for their treasures. A man with talent will be taken advantage of. A woman in love will be introduced to her broken heart. A child at bay will soon no longer see joy. A leader will be questioned. A follower will doubt.

Today I Was Mistaken for a Girl

Maybe it was the way that I dressed
more stylish and intentional
than most guys I knew.

Maybe it was my longer hair
that draped on the side of my head
crooning a style not many used nowadays.

Maybe it was my voice
a little higher pitched
for a young man my height and stature.

There was once a time
if this had happened to me
I would wallow in my manhood
and rethink how I presented myself
to others.

But where one's masculinity might stand on the pillars of ego
and pride
mine stands on the shoulders of compassion and kindness—
as secure as a mother's embrace
as strong as a father's protecting arms.

I'm a man to me
and that's all that matters.

Body of Water

When I get nervous
I take a walk along a body of water—
I smell the breeze and take in the beauty

To calm my brain
I read poetry at the top of my lungs
from my heart to this body of water

In her silence
she speaks to me

She teaches me that I don't have to speak
to teach a heart to heal

Never Stopped

I never stopped loving you
the most beautiful woman
I've laid my eyes on
the kindest heart
that has let me in
a passionate lover
in every sense of the phrase

I never stopped loving you
I only stopped believing
in forever

Time Capsule

My past lovers serve
as the perfect time capsule
allowing me to revisit a day in my mind
and remember the person I used to be—
the person enclosed in their smile
the person that they used to love
the person who saw magic in the world
before the world stole it away

In the Case of Gravity

Gravity can kill you, but it will only do so
when you betray the ground for the sky
when you trade in walking for flying
when you choose dreams over reality

IN BETWEEN

In Between

They say that the most important parts
of a piece of writing are the beginning and the end.
They call it the "power position—"
the beginning being the hook that takes you in,
the end, inspiring a change in the reader.

I really hope this principle, this fundamental, this law of belief
doesn't apply to my life.

I don't want to live just because I began,
I don't want to live just at the end,
I don't want my relevance to be defined by who I was at the start,
or the finish line,
because every other version of myself that lives in between those
two days
are just as relevant.
Somewhere in all the in-between clutter, I was happy.

There exists a gap between Now and Happiness—
a space we think we can fill ourselves,
but that void is too large to fill with an unfinished story,
too large to occupy with our hopes and dreams,
too large to bridge our ideas of Here and Now with Then and
When.

I've seen Happiness and Never have an affair,
and the same goes with Now and Despair.
I've seen people drunk on empty promises
and people high on their scars but no one notices.
How much more do we have to endure
our Happiness taunting us.

There exists a gap between Now and Happiness,
but on some days that gap doesn't seem so large.

Some days it feels like they're just
two people looking for a reason to spark up a conversation;
flint meet steel, you two would be perfect for each other.

Some days Now and Happiness are the ocean and the sky.
They exist worlds apart, but the beauty is found when you live
in between.
You can't fully appreciate a sky when it's blowing through your
soul,
you can't grasp the vastness of the ocean when it pulls at your
lungs,
but when you step back and let Now exist when it should, and
Happiness exist where it may,
you can take in the beauty of being in between.

It's too bad my happiness and yours
live on opposite sides of an indifferent universe.
I hope that one day a black hole can make way
and erase all this space, all this noise,
between my happiness and yours.

With all that being said,
there will still always be a gap
between Now and Happiness
and that's where we exist.

The princes and princesses
The boy in love who second-guesses
The hopeless romantics and the shattered dreamers
Those whose lives once depended on believers
The sum of us who pursue an unforgiving imagination

This is where we exist
In between

So look at yourself in a new light
You are someone's in-between
That very thing
That can bring
Now and Happiness that much closer

THE DREAMER

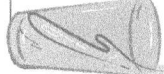

Blank Page

I give you this earnest confession of mine,
I'm a little afraid of this piece of paper
the empty canvas intimidating me with its
textured forefront and a battle of perfection.

Why should one deface
what is already perfect—
the blank page before you?

I'll tell you why.

Because you'll never know the potential,
that'll come from a blank page
if you only let it be
what it already is.

So, start creating,
and see the charm
that is starting something new.

Why I Write

My eyeline skips across the way
as I walk toward the sea wall

Looking for a muse today
an unkempt "be all, end all"

The reason why I live in ink
to capture what I'm feeling

An endless river of borrowed time
in volumes I end up stealing

The introspection that ensures
this collection of carbon atoms

The breath of life imbued
by one's forgotten unsung anthem

The Beautiful Now

Just because I don't close my eyelids as often as I should
because my pupils are glued to this canvas of reality,
it doesn't mean I don't paint with my dreams—
it doesn't mean my toes don't gently kiss the floor at
Christmas Eve—
it doesn't mean I didn't place a tooth under my pillow for the
tooth fairy.

However, the Now is rather different than I had imagined; I've
never been here before.
Being a dreamer, I've always lived on the backs of a little bit
forward—
being a dreamer, I've always travelled on the side stories of fairy
tales—
being a dreamer, I dreamed dreams into existence,
and built pillars to hold my castle, made of what's to come.

But the future leaves more to be desired than the Now,
because in the Now I can exist, in the future I hope to exist—
in the Now I can love, in the future I can only hope I'm given
that chance—
in the Now I can be happy, in the future I might never get
that far—
in the Now you're here, in the future... I hope you're there too.

But, my dear friend,
it is Tomorrow that sustains me;

Tomorrow is a dreamer's paradise—
a place devoid of gravity, and where freedom lies in the realm
of no control.

Yesterday falls into the abyss of déjà vu and the forgotten—
the world where regret lives but memories thrive.

Today is when your footsteps leave more than just footprints,
they become messages to the earth
saying:
  "I exist,"
  "I am living,"
  "I am making my mark."

Maybe this bridge isn't just made with hopeful thoughts for
what comes.
I hope that Tomorrow and Today aren't only connected by these
shoestrings called dreams.
Maybe, just maybe,

You are Today
as I am Tomorrow,
and we are exactly
when we're supposed to be here.
So might you take my hand
and follow me
and we'll be the quills
that write history
for forever.

Something Beautiful

Sometimes I feel like a fraud when I stumble upon a beautiful word on the internet,
as if I'm cheating the mysterious allure that is the way we communicate.
I wonder if I didn't have the internet,
would I be more well-spoken,
or would my words hold less weight?

I want to be able to find beautiful words the way we dream of finding beautiful souls;
I want to meet,
understand,
comprehend,
empathize,
fall in love.

I want that intimacy that comes with finding a word you didn't know, and wondering how in the world did you live without it?

Now that the dictionary is in everything
it no longer serves its purpose,
and the love story, that is, finding something beautiful
is reduced to
a few clicks,
a few swipes,
and a screen.

Creatures of Habit

We fall into ruts—
our footsteps making pathways
for our future selves to walk upon

Going to the same restaurant
ordering the same food
taking the same bus
watching the same shows

Over and over again
becoming slaves to monotony
the parasite of the living

But every now and then
you feel this pull towards the unknown
it tugs at your soul
showing you this new extraordinary path

I patiently live for those moments—
when you decide
today I'm going to take a right instead of a left
today I'm going to wander
into wonder

Welcome Aboard

My bus driver just said
       "welcome aboard"
and in an instant, I became a six-year-old boy

Holding my mother's hand
I stumble atop the yellow sanded steps—
my sneakers become untied
my eyeline shoots to the clouds

I begin to board this spaceship
and with my mother as my guide
maybe we'll land somewhere amazing
maybe we'll land on a planet
that would finally make her smile

Playground

Kings and queens
that's what we were
towering over that citadel made
of wooden columns and steel pipes
as the structure whispered to us
stories of dangerous feats that enticed
all who breathed
it was the danger
that made living worth it

Since such a time when
fear came seldomly
we've stripped away
our wooden and steel kingdom
of its glory

Oh, what a shame it is
to see kingdoms fall

Draws Me to You

The incessant
push and pull
conflict and peace
acting at its finest

This entropy of our universe
is what draws me to you

When Does a Sound Stop?

To us a sound stops when
we can no longer hear it

when the wavelength diminishes
and is blurred by the air around us

when the frequency of a sound
loses its strength to carry on

when our ears give up on
trying to listen

but does a sound ever
really disappear?

What if there's a dimensionless realm
of time and space smaller than the Planck length
where all the "I love yous" ever spoken
find home?

One of These Days

One of these days,
       people are going to hear
       just how amazing she sounds.
       She'll be on that stage,
       despite her age
       unafraid of what she needs to say
       because her music says it all.

One of these days,
       I'm going to have to
       fight the crowd
       for a second with her.

One of these days,
       I'm going to have to
       stop time
       for a day with her.

One of these days,
       she'll walk down the street
       as if God paved this road,
       built this room, made this world
       just for her.

One of these days,
>   I'll check the attic of my mind
>   where I stored all the memories of the past.
>   I'll dust off the shelves, put on a record
>   and slow dance in the dark.

One of these days,
>   I'll open a box
>   marked "old dreams"
>   and remember what she smelt of.

One of these days,
>   she's going to outgrow me
>   like an old sweater
>   and forget why
>   she kept me around all this time.

One of these days,
>   all I will be
>   is a loose thread to her.
>   But at least I would know,
>   there was a time
>   when I kept her warm.

Playlist

Love was a song, and every past lover of mine was a rhyme
until the day I met you and saw how
a melody could redefine its horizons
to allow love to live as a playlist to be desired

Iced Green Tea Latte

To the cute barista
at that cafe
everyone talks about
that's only a bus ride from my house

I order an iced green tea latte every time I come
hoping you'll one day take my order
interrupt me and say
"iced green tea latte?"

You'll never know my name
and I'll never know yours—
you're just a cute stranger
I enjoy conversing with, in my head
while I pretend that the world around me doesn't turn

You Can Choose the Record This Time

Share with me the
sweetness of this music

Enjoy the collective activity
of our souls swirling about the room
gliding on the fervent sounds
that were born before our time

Purist

You don't have to be an expert to speak about the affairs of the heart
You don't have to be a professional to enjoy what life has to offer
You don't have to be a purist to give ground for your ideas to walk on
Dip your toes into everything and let knowledge carry you
Aim your burning passion into the depths of humanity and let it guide you in the eve of life
Grasp onto something meaningful and let it give shape to your existence
You are a silhouette of bones, and blood, and skin, and flesh
You are sculpture of multiple mediums—
Nothing about you is pure
But everything about you is beautiful

Thoughts

It's amusing how some thoughts find a way to stick around
Like the name of the tallest living man
that book you never returned to the library
that time you thought it was a good idea to wear your sister's
jeans to school

These pockets of memories just floating
never forgotten
keeping alive
a past that no one else remembers

Silence

We don't embrace silence enough,
filling every void in a dialogue
like a dumpster truck filling in
the cracks of cement,
with garbage conversations—
useless information.

We don't embrace silence enough,
it's like we're embarrassed
at being speechless
when some of the most incredible parts of our world
are the thieves of our words.
Kissing the woman you love, for the first time,
witnessing a newborn find out what breathing is like,
standing at the top of a mountain as you let your wonder settle.

These moments carry silence on their backs
just the same as others do.

So, the next time you find yourself
trapped in the middle of two silent voices,
I hope you smile at the fact
that all the noise in the world
is no longer there
to distract you,
from what's in front of you.

Astigmatism

The streetlights painted the roads
with streaks that resembled dying stars

As we drove into the night
it felt warm, as if the light were holding my face
and as I squinted, it poured into my vision like a rushing river—
the bokeh born from my cornea, adorned with images of
dancing lights

It's a fascinating power
to have the ability to see beauty
in the darkness

She Did More than Just Click a Button

The intent of a photographer
is not one that should be overlooked

As photographers
we are thieves scattered amongst history
stealing moments from time and in doing so

we've betrayed the split second that lives in between
an instant, and non-existent
and have learned to stretch *that*
into eternity

To My Dance Teacher

You didn't teach me how to dance,
I'm confident in that fact
I think on some level
we all already knew how to do that

Instead, you taught me
how to lose myself
in the things I loved

Movement was just the language
you taught me in

Spotlight

The sun shines only when the sun shines
it never steals the sky from the moon

The moon on the other hand
every so often
is allowed to share the sky with her friend

Sunset

It wasn't the first break of evening I've ever experienced,
it certainly wasn't the first time the sun said goodbye to me
while the pale blue turned in its bed to reveal its back of
evening sky
and yet it was still the most captivating sunset I had ever seen,
but what was so different?

The warmth wrapped my cheeks,
plump and cold,
as the wind tried to undo
the impression the sun left on me.

Why was this one so unlike the others?

The glare on my glasses began to create
streams of light across my cornea
and as the particles fled in, so did an epiphany.
This friend of a sunset lit the sombre of heartbreak
ablaze within me to align our understandings,
and as he did so, he spoke of a lesson:
that anything worthwhile
has an ending—

The year
the month
the day
and every moment amidst it all.

Crucible

The mountains form
somewhat of a wall
protecting these years
I've stolen for myself

Allowing these twenties
to ignite the change to come
brought forth by my
hands alone

Therefore, I must guard
my youthfulness alongside
these mountainous horizons
so that I might craft
a crucible within the confines
of this city that
belongs to me

He'll Keep You Company

You're riding a one-way train to who knows where—

You're on this train with strangers
the passengers who were part of your past
crew members guiding you forward
and you end up in an empty car
watching as the leaves grace the windows with their colour
streaks of light pass you by too quickly to comprehend

Your youth is stripped from you
as time creeps up your legs
slowly reaching your face
and an older gentleman appears in place
of the younger one that was just there

But despite it all
the wide-eyed dreamer child still lives here
he'll keep you company
reminding you
to never stop dreaming
on this train
to who knows where

To the Guy on My Bus Wearing Too Much Cologne

You cannot buy manliness
It isn't something that can come from a bottle
it is something you learn to be

We are not born men
we are born boys—
clueless
stupid
and ignorant

Very few of us grow out of this—
those of us who do
still wander, seeking answers
in other flawed men

It is useless to try and prove to me
your bravado
with your headache-inducing scent

The Riddle in the Mirror

I'm puzzled by the riddle in the mirror written in false masculinity
because amongst the larger muscles and broader shoulders
beyond the taller stature and forgone composure
I see sparse remnants of a little boy
wanting so badly
to be a man

Headfirst

It's not that I know more than you do
when I speak about
the affairs of the heart

It's that I sleep on a bed of thoughts
and I let them consume me
as I drift into the void

It's that I give safe passage for
meaning to travel through
my veins and arteries

It's that I dive headfirst into feeling
and drown my lungs
in introspection

While *you* hold your breath
and swim to the surface

Just a Dream

There's a glint of doubt in your eyes
when I speak of my dreams in your presence
and this is what I say to that—

It's okay if it's just a dream
it doesn't owe reality anything

The First

She was the first girl—
She somehow was always the first

She was the first "ily" and the first "I love you."
She was the first hand hold, tight hug, and goodnight text
She was the first written song, poem said and note passed
She was the first safe house, heartbreak and first kiss
She was the first drunk call, farewell and morning bliss

She was the first hug I received at a party, and the first to ever
see me in a crowd
She was the first girl who was taller than me, and the first one
who saw me as proud
She was the first heart I learned how to break, the first lesson of
love's tremor and quake
She was the first person to accept my demons, but I still regret
letting her see them

But firsts only last once—
The first can never be first
The second time around

Therefore, I hold her in regretful remiss
For she taught me of love's wonder—
A debt I hope to repay

The Second

She was the unrequited love—
an unopened Pandora's box of feelings
she was a friend on the surface
but in her presence my heart fluttered

This girl was the main character in her own movie
and the love interest in mine
if only I had mustered up the courage
to reveal such a thought to her back then
instead of letting the melancholy surround me

Years later, and here I am modelling a purple heart, one that
was weathered and tired
she and I have a conversation as arbitrary and aleatory as they
had always been
we're caught on a streamlined wind of popcorn thoughts—
banter bouncing about the room—
I told her I liked her once upon a time
and there was a glisten in her eye when she said she had once
felt the same

It was like this road of time that I've been running on
had been the wrong turn in a series of wrong turns
and this VHS of reality was interrupted by a foggy dream
in which my life and hers had collided a bit differently

But I see that she's happy—
a good man at her side that makes her smile
but even so it's still fun to live in a different reality—
live in this dream even just for a while

The Third

She treated me with more kindness than I ever deserved
She was the best friend I didn't realize I needed
She was awkward and spoke a little too much
But was interesting and fun to listen to
She taught me that love takes effort and is complicated
That love doesn't have to be first kisses and holding hands
Love can be the songs we sang
Love could be the memories we made when we dated
Love can be innocent, pure and unadulterated—
That our bodies were no substitute for time
She gave me hers and I gave her mine
She showed me that balloons weren't filled with helium gas
But were filled with the things that we loved about each other
The levity in our love brought us together

I don't remember ever explicitly telling her I loved her
I don't think she ever told me either

I do know that I met a beautiful soul
Someone's story that intertwined with mine
In some strange way

The Last

At the end of time, if I had to
I would peel back the surface of the sun
to find evidence of *The Last*
I would search the oceans
and allow the pressure to grind my cells into a pulp
if it meant I could find a piece of her at the bottom

Love is quite a strange feeling
and my love for her was no different;
a difficult undertaking, yes, but if love were easy
I don't think it would clutch onto history like it has—
the language of romance dancing from poetry to cinema
like an unlawful bandit
stealing too many hearts to count

Love brought me to the mirror every morning
to allow the monologues in my chest
to rehearse their performance
for when I met her for the first time
the evening when it all began
a whirlpool worth yielding to

Our story went like this:
we met, a far from perfect meet cute
became friends, an unconventional pair
walked away, in search of something different
fell in love, an alluring force unbroken
fell apart, slowly transforming us into a tragic sentence
that ended in an ellipsis

And alas here we are
the end of an amusing tale retold—
the one that did not last
and the last one that I had loved
might just be *The Last*

An Endless Road

I try to close my eyes so that I can
remember what home feels like;
it feels like your soft fingers running down
the miles and miles of skin along my back

As I look out onto the coast
I see the thin line where the sky meets the ocean
the endless horizon holding them together
before the physical bounds of existence pull them apart

I wonder if they miss each other just as I miss you

If only the shutter of my eyelids
could shape reality and create
the imaginary horizon that
binds two beings like us
that exist miles away from each other

When I close my eyes
I can be where I want to be

When I close my eyes
I see my love in bed with me

When I close my eyes
I feel her touch on my face

When I close my eyes
home is never too far away

Without Me

When we met
I saw how the world
tricked you into thinking
that you could never love again

I had the pleasure of witnessing
your eyes flood with dreams—

Dreams that water
the seeds we planted together

I saw how you learned to love again
I hope you remember that feeling

The euphoria that comes with falling in love and know
if you could relearn once with me
you could do it again without me

Mother to My Poems

You were the mother to my poems
the spark to this ferocity of passion
the catalyst of this ever-growing
garden of metaphors

But it was our end that
pushed me to write down the words
that crowded my mind
to give room to understanding
just who you are in this narrative of mine

A Lie I Told You

When I was younger the phrase
"think before you speak"
was sung at every opportunity
my mouth became a drainpipe—
unfiltered and raw.

From then on, I was always careful with the words I spoke.
It was in those moments
of my dissolving childhood
when I became a writer.
Only I did not do so on paper—
I wrote stanzas and paragraphs,
essays and speeches
in the confines of my mind,
archived in the form of
conversations and stories,
lies and excuses,
dreams and ambitions.

Back then, I said the words
"I will love you as long as you'll let me"
as a cautionary excuse
for the future me to use—
a contingency just in case
the love story we had written
would end in a simmering smoke
fleeing from the wick of a candle.

What I did not know then,
I do know now.

My love for you has never been
a causality of your permission,
but an undying fact
until my final breath.

Drowning

I drowned myself in poetry and books
      to block out the constant hum of
          your voice that rings in my heart.
              I saw the skid before it happened,
         so I leaned into the crash
     giving in to life's undoing,
   hoping that by submitting to the river
      I could at least steer with the current.
         I was not prepared to be consumed into
             this shipwreck of existence.
        So I drowned, I disappeared, I died.
     But even death could not swallow my sorrows,
which then led me to wash up on this shore.
   I lifted myself with the heavyset absence of you,
      cut my veins with words
         and bled myself out in metaphors.
           I spilt it all on these pages
      that I hope you'll read one day.

Through Midnight

I crash into midnight like a boat in a storm
any second and I'll tip over and sink into sleep

My eyelids peel back as I battle with darkness
my breathing catching on the silence—

And as my chest presses onto my lungs
the captain of my consciousness
whispers
"hold on we're almost there"

Like a Storm

My imagination   has   betrayed me
As   I walk into oblivion

It feels familiar
Like   a daydream   but different

I   can feel it   burrow into my chest
As I curl up   into   a ball

Thinking,   if I'm small enough
There won't be   enough of me   to hurt

The air   in my lungs,   afraid to leave
The   air around me,   too scared to enter

My mind   tethered   to ideas   made of faulty parachutes
Blowing in different   directions

My thoughts become a broken record
Skipping   on the cracks   of my exterior

It's   like a storm   I can't escape

Through Your Fingertips

Consciousness floods   in
destroying   the world you've   created.
     You sift through the   wreckage

        searching   for   some
         unknown treasure,

      or it might be a key   you're   looking for—
       a key to a safe filled   with stories.
           You catch glimpses
            of a life you lived
      when the universe was   silent.

Now tell me: what in the world
was that dream about?

How It Would Go

The plummet

The fall

The sound of cars screaming at the sidewalks
and painted lines
all blurred by the furious wind rushing you unrelentingly

The prickling spikes of the mid evening frost
scraping your cheeks with no remorse
leaving impressions of red—
separating skin—
convincing blood to run away to their hiding places

You try and fight the instinct to close your eyes
uneasy tears
born from not only the cold
but also regret

What used to be a welcoming body of water
now seems like a dark abyss
that you've let yourself
fall into

And at the moment before oblivion
there is only one thing you miss
more than your mother's face
and that is
the edge of that bridge
you so desperately remember
being the last thing of this world
to let you go

Apocalyptic

I think if the world were to end tomorrow
humanity crumbling to a halt in the face
of some cataclysmic event

I think the list of the things we regret doing
would be much smaller than
the list of things we regret *not* doing

Form

If life is the glass, and I am the water,
so it would seem that I should take its
shape. But although I may not be
the master of my form I am still
allowed to be what I am—
I can still be the water,
ever adaptable, yet
unchanged.

With Faulty Hands

Dr. A. R. Dykes once said that structural engineering is
    "the art of moulding materials we do not wholly understand,
    into shapes we cannot precisely analyse,
    so as to withstand forces we cannot really assess."
We build such great structures
with faulty hands.

You'd think we would have more confidence
in our ability to take care
of the people around us, yet
    we love people with feelings we can't quite comprehend,
    bring them through a life too chaotic to predict,
    in hopes to prove that forever exists.

Like building structures meant to live in,
Love has no real reason of lasting,
but like all the greatest structural engineers in history,
a hopeless romantic like myself must take that leap of faith,
to prove that
the greatest structure ever built—
the greatest Love I've ever had,
can last.

When We Depart

If life is a painting
and you and I
are just these brush strokes
gracing the canvas—
we'll be too close to even see
the significance of the footsteps we leave

But I'm betting when our bristles depart
from this still life that we've created
to look in awe of the marks we've left—

My best guess is that
it'll look like something
that was worth living

Rest Well

On my deathbed
do not ask me
for my final words
or a goodbye hug

Instead, give me
a pen and paper
so that I can draw you a
map of where I'm headed

Or maybe I'll begin to write you
my last poem, so that you
can give it an ending that earns
the right to rest well

Acknowledgements

This book would not have been possible without the few people who allowed me to share with them my heart in words. Thank you to Ralph Aguila, Karl Ocampo, Jacqueline Realina, Danielle Coronado, Camille Dansereau, Jay Legaspi, Anamica Sunderaswara, and Glisha Dela Cruz for giving these poems room to breathe and the countless amount of support and input that allowed this book to become what it is today. A special thank you to Mary Clarin for editing this slice of my life and helping me improve my craft, and to my good friend and illustrator Jewel Dimaya for always going above and beyond in the things we create together. A large debt of my gratitude also goes to the team at Tellwell Publishing for guiding me through this arduous process of self-publishing. Being a STEM major, publishing my first book has been a daunting experience and one that needed different tools than what I'm used to using, and I owe it to these people for inspiring me every step of the way as I made this dream a reality.

Thank you to my family for showing me what it really takes to survive this strange world we live in. It's because of the lessons you instilled in me that I was able to craft tools to speak my truth. You showed me that my purpose on this earth can be found in whatever direction I walked towards. I will never forget the abundance of faith you have in me, and how that faith has changed my life.

I wanted to acknowledge the handful of friends who have stuck by my side through my recent years of heartbreak, introspection, and self-discovery. To Danielle Coronado, a lover turned friend, and a symbol of how love can endure. To Marcus Flores and Paolo Mata for being an unstoppable force of brotherhood—it's your presence and absence that keeps me going. To Patricia Macapagal and Tobi Agonias, my creative counterparts and an extension of my passion for the arts. To Kate Alcazar, a fellow misfit, romantic and an image of strength in my life. To Nolan Conley and Cole Stainer, two wonderful dreamers that I found while finding myself. And to Glisha Dela Cruz for reminding me everyday how precious life can be when you allow yourself to be in love.

I also wanted to thank *you*
for picking up this book
and with every page you turned
you breathed life into the words I wrote.

CPSIA information can be obtained
at www.ICGtesting.com
Printed in the USA
LVHW050737040522
717735LV00002B/367

9 780228 864165